W9-BZX-723
Captain LaPasta
Barnabas Brambles
S.S. SPAGHETTI
Leo
Sir Sidney
Old Coal

THIS BOOK
BELONGS TO:

OTHER BOOKS WRITTEN BY **KATE KLISE**
AND ILLUSTRATED BY **M. SARAH KLISE**

Three-Ring Rascals
The Show Must Go On!
The Greatest Star on Earth

43 Old Cemetery Road
Dying to Meet You
Over My Dead Body
Till Death Do Us Bark
The Phantom of the Post Office
Hollywood, Dead Ahead
Greetings from the Graveyard
The Loch Ness Punster

Regarding the Fountain
Regarding the Sink
Regarding the Trees
Regarding the Bathrooms
Regarding the Bees

Letters from Camp
Trial by Journal

Shall I Knit You a Hat?
Why Do You Cry?
Imagine Harry
Little Rabbit and the Night Mare
Little Rabbit and the Meanest Mother on Earth
Stand Straight, Ella Kate
Grammy Lamby and the Secret Handshake

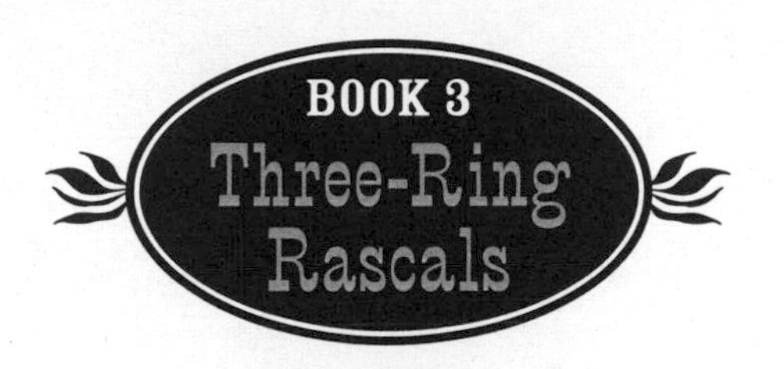

THE CIRCUS GOES to SEA

KATE KLISE

ILLUSTRATED BY

M. SARAH KLISE

ALGONQUIN YOUNG READERS • 2014

Published by
Algonquin Young Readers
An imprint of Algonquin Books of Chapel Hill
P.O. Box 2225
Chapel Hill, North Carolina 27515-2225

a division of
Workman Publishing
225 Varick Street
New York, New York 10014

Printed in the United States of America.
Published simultaneously in Canada by Thomas Allen & Son Limited.
Design by M. Sarah Klise.

LIBRARY OF CONGRESS CATALOGING-IN-PUBLICATION DATA
Klise, Kate.
The circus goes to sea / by Kate Klise ; illustrated by M. Sarah Klise.
pages cm.—(Three-ring rascals ; book 3)
Summary: Many surprises are in store when Miss Flora Endora Eliza LaBuena LaPasta invites Sir Sidney's Circus to travel and perform aboard her elegant ship, the SS *Spaghetti*.
ISBN 978-1-61620-365-8
[1. Circus—Fiction. 2. Ships—Fiction. 3. Ocean travel—Fiction.]
I. Klise, M. Sarah, illustrator. II. Title.
PZ7.K684Cir 2014
[Fic]—dc23 2014014703

10 9 8 7 6 5 4 3 2 1
First Edition

This book is dedicated to our nieces,

Flora and *Eliza*.

THE CIRCUS GOES to SEA

No matter how big the sea may be,
sometimes two ships meet.

—Chinese Proverb

CHAPTER ONE

By now you've surely heard of Sir Sidney's Circus. Maybe you've even been to see a show.

If so, you know that Sir Sidney's Circus is the best circus in the whole wide world. Many people wait all year for the Sir Sidney Circus train to arrive in their town.

Some fans come to the circus to see Elsa the elephant.

Other people prefer to listen to Leo the lion and Tiger the kitten.

Everyone *ooohs* and *aaahs* when the Famous Flying Banana Brothers perform their tricks on the trapeze.

For some time now, Sir Sidney has been helping Barnabas Brambles, ringmaster-in-training, be a better man. Every day they meet for a lesson. Barnabas Brambles has many questions.

Can I lie?
Can I cheat?
Can I steal from children?
Can I be mean to animals?
Can I be a bully?
Can I be greedy?
Can I be greedy
if I say *please*?

"What *can* I do?" Barnabas Brambles asked Sir Sidney one day not long ago. "There's nothing left."

"Yes there is," said Sir Sidney. "You can be *kind*. Just try to be kind to everyone you meet. The world will change when you open your heart to others."

Bert and Gert were in their mouse hole, listening to every word. "Sir Sidney is so wise," said Gert. "He speaks like a poet." A bright idea popped into Gert's head. "We should write a book of poems."

"Poems?" said Bert. "I don't want to write a book of poems. I hate poetic stuff and all that lovey-dovey fluff."

Gert giggled at her brother's rhyme. "Poems don't have to be about love," she said. "You can write a poem about anything. Watch this."

She put a piece of paper in her typewriter. Gert loved the tiny machine, even though the *i* key sometimes stuck. She used her claws to tap out a quick poem.

```
I think my brother is a poet.
Problem is, he doesn't know it.
```

Bert shook his head when he saw what his sister had written.

I am *not* a poet. Not now, not ever. I'd rather write a book of jokes.
MY JOKES

Barnabas Brambles was feeling frustrated, too.

I don't think I *can* be kind. Not now, not *ever.* But I'm glad you're my teacher, Sir Sidney.
Let the circus be your teacher. Everything you need to know is right here. Just stick with us. You'll learn plenty.

As they were talking, Old Coal flew through the window. The black bird was another member of Sir Sidney's Circus. Her job was to deliver mail to and from the circus.

As usual, Old Coal carried a letter in her beak. She dropped it into Sir Sidney's hands. The circus owner looked at the envelope. He didn't recognize the return address. He opened the letter and read it out loud.

Flora Endora Eliza LaBuena LaPasta

Aboard the SS *Spaghetti*

November 3

Sir Sidney
Owner and Founder
Sir Sidney's Circus
Somewhere in the USA

Dear Sir Sidney,

I would like to invite your circus to be my guests aboard the SS *Spaghetti*. The *Spaghetti* is a floating palace of elegance and entertainment. It also happens to be my home.

I hope you can join me on the ship's next voyage. We will depart New York City at eleven o'clock in the morning on November 4. (That's tomorrow.)

Sincerely,

Flora Endora Eliza LaBuena LaPasta

When Sir Sidney finished reading the letter, Barnabas Brambles clapped his hands and clicked his heels together. "Boy-man-howdy!" he said. "Aren't we the luckiest ducks that ever clucked? We're going on a cruise! We'd better pack our bags immediately."

"It's more serious than that," said Sir Sidney, rubbing his belly. "I get terribly sick whenever I travel by water. Just thinking about being on a ship makes my stomach do somersaults. We'll have to say no to Miss LaPasta's invitation."

But Barnabas Brambles wasn't listening. He was yelling to the others on the train.

When everyone was gathered, Barnabas Brambles reread Miss LaPasta's letter out loud for all to hear. He was smiling like a jack-o'-lantern. "Can you imagine the fun we could have on a cruise? We'll be a floating circus."

Barnabas Brambles waved away all their concerns as if he were waving away a harmless fly. "Why are you so worried? Where's your sense of adventure?" Then he lowered his voice. "Don't you *get* it? This is the opportunity of a lifetime. Big things happen when you take a chance."

Leo looked at Barnabas Brambles.

Why are you so eager to go to sea?
Have you ever been on a ship?
Never. But ever since I was a little boy I've wanted to go to sea.

"Aw! Aw!" Old Coal cried. Barnabas Brambles laughed at the crow. "Did you think I'd forget you? No way. You're coming with us, Old Coal. We wouldn't go without our favorite fine-feathered friend."

But the crow repeated herself. "Aw! Aw!" She flew over to Sir Sidney's desk and tapped Miss LaPasta's letter with her beak.

"What do you think Old Coal is trying to say?" Gert whispered to Bert.

"I don't know," said Bert. "But there's only one way to find out." He took a deep breath and then sprinted up Sir Sidney's desk. Gert followed right behind. They looked like the world's tiniest mountain climbers.

"Look," said Bert when they reached the top of the desk. "There's something else in this envelope."

"It's another piece of paper," said Gert. "Let's pull it out so Sir Sidney can see it."

"What's this?" asked Sir Sidney when he saw what the mice had done. "It looks like I missed something." He picked up the second piece of paper and read the words on it. His face looked troubled.

What is it?
A *postscriptum* from Miss LaPasta.
What's a *postscriptum*?
Postscriptum is Latin for "written after." We usually abbreviate it to P.S. You can add a P.S. after you've written a letter. It's a way of adding a final thought.

"Let me see what it says," said Barnabas Brambles, grabbing the paper away from Sir Sidney. He read the P.S. in a loud voice so everyone could hear.

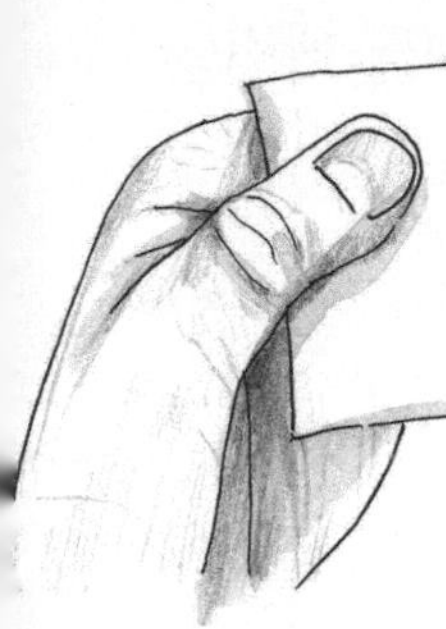

P.S. I would prefer that Barnabas Brambles ***not*** join us on this voyage. I've heard he's the meanest man alive.

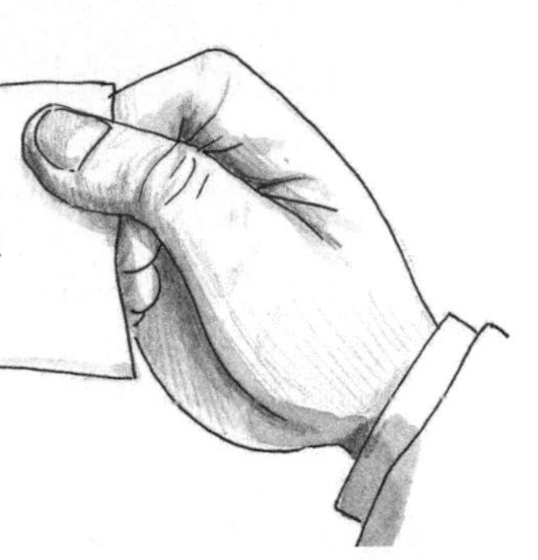

In an instant, Barnabas Brambles's smile turned upside down. The happiness he had felt a minute earlier was replaced by a heavy disappointment that sat like a sandbag in his stomach. He could say only one word: "Oh."

"Oh indeed," said Sir Sidney with a sigh. "I guess that settles it. We're going to sea."

"Send me a postcard," Barnabas Brambles mumbled glumly.

"That won't be necessary," said Sir Sidney. "You're coming with us."

"But Miss LaPasta doesn't want me to come," said Barnabas Brambles. "She said so in her P.S."

"I know," said Sir Sidney. "And that's exactly why you *are* coming. I want Miss Flora Endora Eliza LaBuena LaPasta to see what a fine man you're becoming. Now pack your bags, everyone. The circus is going to sea."

CHAPTER TWO

That night Sir Sidney and his circus traveled to New York. They arrived in Manhattan the next morning, just as the sun was coming up.

Just then the train made a turn and crossed a bridge. A spectacular vision appeared on the horizon.

As Sir Sidney pulled the train up to the dock, he spotted a sign.

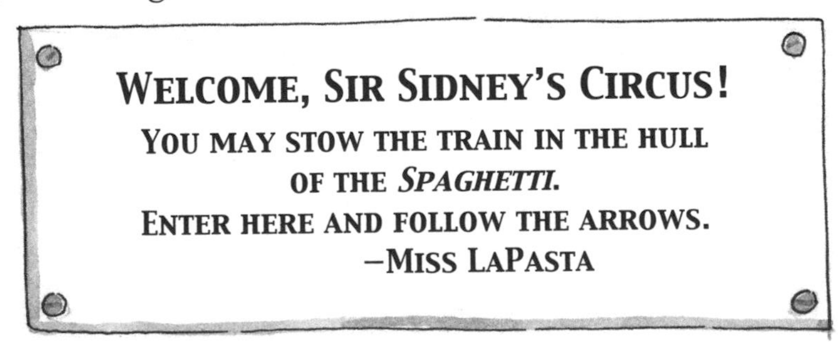

WELCOME, SIR SIDNEY'S CIRCUS!
YOU MAY STOW THE TRAIN IN THE HULL OF THE *SPAGHETTI*.
ENTER HERE AND FOLLOW THE ARROWS.
–MISS LAPASTA

The train slowly glided into the belly of the enormous ship. Everyone piled out with suitcases and traveling bags.

"This way!" called Barnabas Brambles. He pointed to another sign that signaled a staircase.

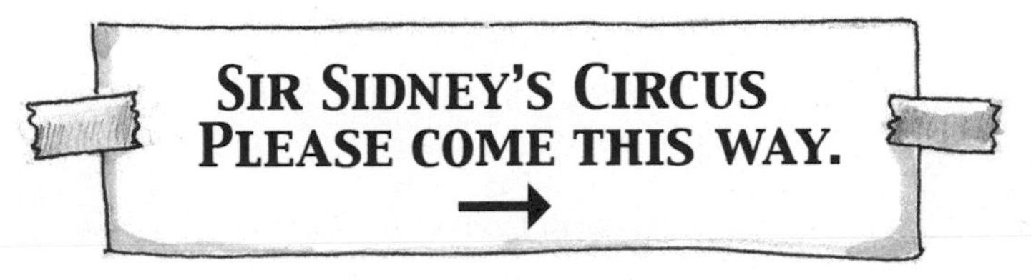

As the members of Sir Sidney's Circus were going up the stairs, several people were coming down. They were carrying large trunks.

"Problem?" repeated Barnabas Brambles with a wide smile. He was feeling too happy to let anyone spoil his good mood. "How can there be a problem when you're on a ship as majestic as the SS *Spaghetti*?"

Because we all just got *fired.* Miss LaPasta wants a whole *new* crew of entertainers. Something about bananas and brothers.
Oh.
I see.
Miss LaPasta said she wanted cute, furry animals, too.
Mraare.
Miss LaPasta must be very important.

"That's one word for her," said the woman in the sparkly dress. "I can think of other words. You'll find out when you meet her."

Just then the ship's whistle sounded a long blast.

Sir Sidney clutched his stomach as the ship left the harbor.

"Are you seasick already?" asked Elsa.

"Not exactly," said Sir Sidney. "But I have a bad feeling about this trip. I'm concerned about Miss LaPasta and her plans for—"

Before he could finish his sentence, a young girl interrupted him.

"Hello," she said quietly. She was holding a monogrammed scarf.

Look at the letters on her scarf!

At first, everyone was speechless. Finally, Elsa asked the question everyone was thinking.

Are *you* Miss Flora Endora Eliza LaBuena LaPasta?
I am. You were expecting someone older?

"Or at least *bigger*," said Leo. "Your name is very big."

"My mother says I'll grow into it," said the girl, staring at her shoes. She had a sad and lonely look in her eyes, as if she'd never had a friend in her life.

"I am," the girl replied. "You probably think I tricked you into coming. I suppose I did. But I've always wanted to see a circus. I've never seen one. My mother never lets me leave this ship."

Sir Sidney rubbed his chin. "Where *is* your mother?"

"At the helm," said the girl. "She's very busy. And when she finds out I've invited a circus aboard the *Spaghetti*, she'll be furious."

As soon as she said the word *furious*, a thunderous cry rang out.

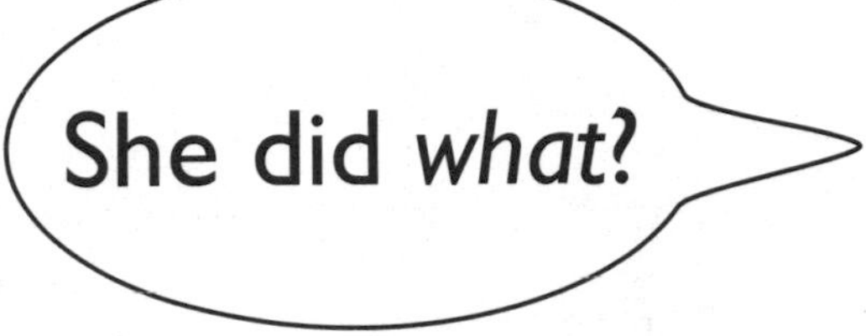

She did *what*?
A *circus*?
That's my mother.
Is that your mother, too?
Uh-huh.
Something tells me your mother isn't thrilled we're here.

They all listened to the sound of heavy footsteps approaching.

Clomp

Clomp

Clomp

Captain Astrid Amanda Miranda LaBuena LaPasta looked even angrier than she sounded.

Flora Endora Eliza LaBuena LaPasta, *explain* yourself!
Ever since I was a little girl I've wanted to see a circus.
So you *fired* our entertainers and invited these . . . *creatures*?

"I didn't invite them all," Flora said in her defense. "I didn't ask Barnabas Brambles to come. He has a terrible reputation."

Barnabas Brambles? I've heard of him. Isn't he the meanest man alive?
I *was*. But that was before I joined the circus.
Now he's getting nicer.
A tiny bit nicer.

Sir Sidney folded his hands together. "May I make a suggestion?" he said calmly. "It seems there's been a misunderstanding. You don't want us here, and some of us don't want to be here. We will disembark, if you'll kindly just turn this ship around and—"

"Turn the ship around?" cried Captain LaPasta. "The *Spaghetti* has never turned back! I don't believe in even *looking* back. You and your crew of carnival workers will disembark at our first port of call."

"Fine," said Sir Sidney. "Where will that be?"

"London, England," replied Captain LaPasta.

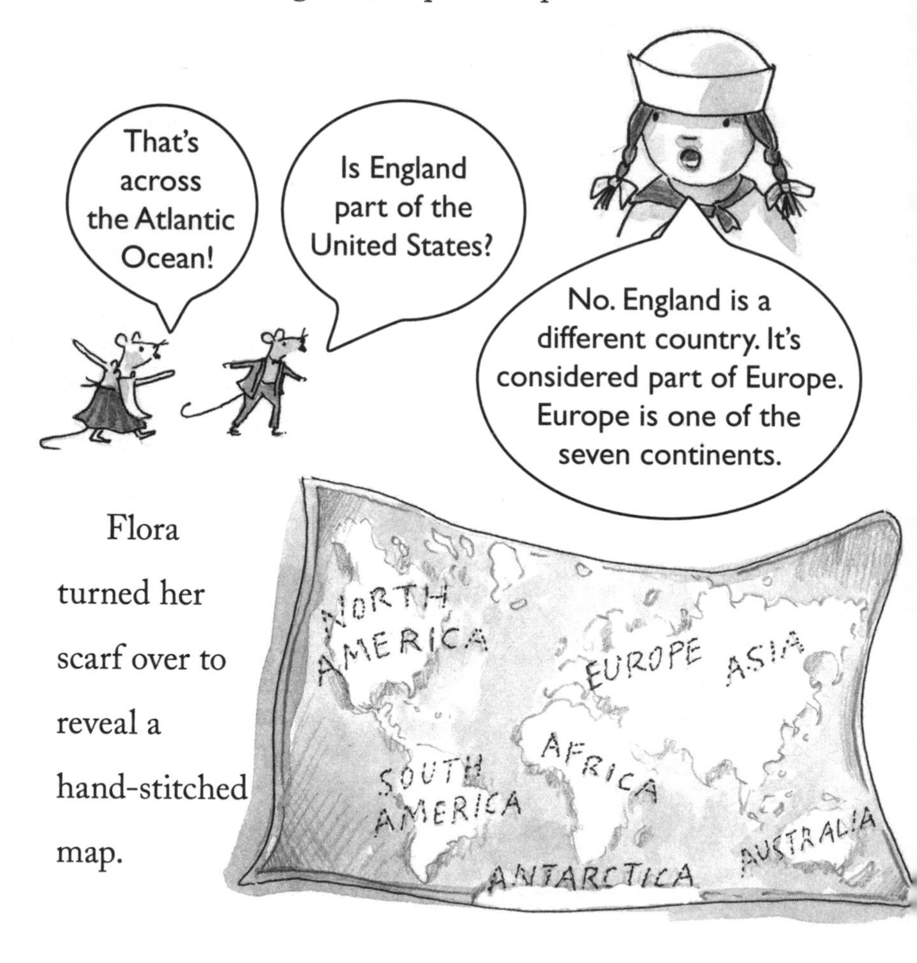

That's across the Atlantic Ocean!
Is England part of the United States?
No. England is a different country. It's considered part of Europe. Europe is one of the seven continents.
NORTH AMERICA
EUROPE
ASIA
AFRICA
SOUTH AMERICA
AUSTRALIA
ANTARCTICA

Flora turned her scarf over to reveal a hand-stitched map.

How long will it take us to get to London by sea?

Sir Sidney used a pen and a scrap of paper to calculate how many hours that would be.

One week = 7 days
1 day = 24 hours
So a weeklong trip is

24 hours
x 7 days

168 hours!

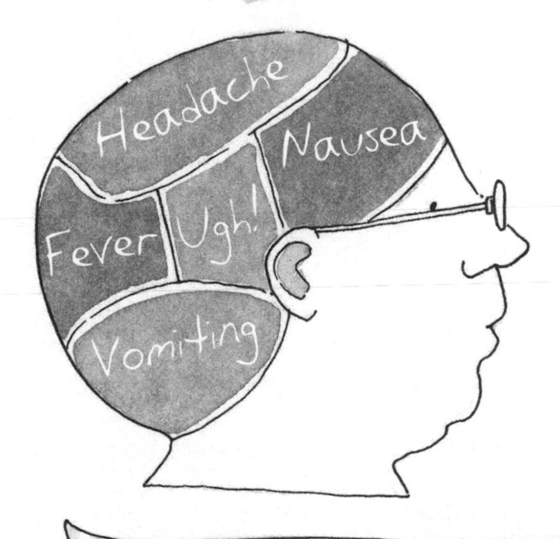

In his brain he began to think what the week ahead would be like.

My Life for the Next 168 Hours

Captain LaPasta had her own concerns. "Passengers on the SS *Spaghetti* pay a lot of money for their tickets," she said to herself. "They expect to see first-class shows every evening. Now that my daughter has fired our regular performers, how will I entertain my guests?"

In her brain she began to think what the week ahead would be like.

Barnabas Brambles was watching with a funny feeling in his stomach. A thin grin sneaked across his lips.

"What are *you* smiling about?" Captain LaPasta demanded.

Barnabas Brambles shrugged. "I'm not sure," he said. He felt his stomach turn a cartwheel. "Maybe I'm getting seasick."

I don't know, but I think I'd better learn how to write a love poem.
Love? Oh no. I'm *doomed.*

But he didn't *feel* sick. He felt a little bit odd and a big bit wonderful.

"What's up with him?" Bert asked his sister.

"I've never been on a cruise," Barnabas Brambles said with a nervous giggle.

"A *cruise*?" Captain LaPasta said, throwing back her shoulders. "This is *not* a *cruise*. We are making a *crossing*. We are traveling from one continent to another across the mighty Atlantic Ocean. Are you ready?"

"I've been waiting for this my whole life," said Barnabas Bramble. His stomach turned another cartwheel.

"Very well then," replied Captain LaPasta. She lifted her chin and spoke in a loud, clear voice.

CHAPTER THREE

Later that day after everyone had unpacked, Flora told the members of Sir Sidney's Circus about her life.

“I was,” said Flora. “But I was also very young. I don’t really have any memories of my father. For most of my life, it’s been just my mother and me—and this enormous ocean.”

Flora leaned in close. “That’s Mr. and Mrs. Slimskin, Mrs. Prunejam, and Mr. Marshmuffin,” she whispered. “They’re all very nice people.”

“But they’re *grown-ups,*” said Elsa.

“Exactly,” said Flora. “They don’t want to play with me. Do you see any passengers *my* age? Do you see anyone who could be *my* friend? I don’t have a brother, a sister, or even a cute, furry animal. I’m growing up alone in the middle of a big, lonely ocean.”

"But my dear girl," said Barnabas Brambles, "you get to live on a *ship*. I can't think of a happier existence."

"I can," said Flora sadly. "I'd rather have a friend."

I'll be your friend.
Aw! Aw!
Me, too!
We can all be your friends.
Mrrare.

"You can count on us," said Barnabas Brambles.

"Thank you," said Flora. "That means a lot to me."

The conversation was interrupted by an announcement.

"Attention. This is your captain speaking. Lunch is being served. Please make your way to the dining room."

The lunch buffet was impressive. It was all prepared by the ship's cook, whose name was Cookie. Because this was the SS *Spaghetti*, Cookie served spaghetti with meatballs from an enormous bowl he wheeled around the dining room on a cart the size of a bed.

Sir Sidney took one look at the buffet and felt sick to his stomach. He stumbled back to his cabin to rest. But all the other passengers loaded their plates high with food.

"Now *this* is living," said Bert, slurping spaghetti.

"You shouldn't overeat," warned Gert. "You'll get indigestion."

"Don't worry," said Flora. "We'll wait one hour before we go swimming."

"Swimming?" asked Leo and Elsa at the same moment.

"Mrrare?" added Tiger.

"I'll teach you," said Flora.

"I don't think I *can* swim," said Gert.

"Me, either," said Bert. "Let me off at the next bus stop."

"There are no buses in the ocean," said Stan Banana.

"Or cars or roads or streets," added Dan Banana.

"If there are no streets, there are no street addresses," said Gert with a puzzled expression on her furry face. She scratched her ears. "Without addresses, how do you know where anything is in the ocean?"

“Excellent question,” Flora said. She took a meatball and wrapped several strands of spaghetti around it.

Think of this as latitude. Latitude lines run horizontally between the North and South Poles, parallel to one another and the equator.

“Now,” said Flora, “think of this as longitude.” She wrapped a second meatball with spaghetti in a vertical direction.

Lines of longitude all begin and end at the North Pole and South Poles. They wrap the entire earth from north to south. See?

"I've never seen lines on Earth going up and down like that," said Stan Banana pointing at one meatball.

"Or back and forth like that," added Dan Banana, pointing at the other meatball.

"Lines of latitude and longitude are *imaginary* lines," said Flora. "They're helpful in describing where things are. Latitude describes the location going north to south. The location is called a coordinate. Longitude describes the coordinate from east to west. If you know both coordinates, you can pinpoint the location of anything, even in the ocean."

Where are we now?
Our approximate location is latitude forty degrees north, longitude seventy-two degrees west.
Golly, she's smart.
Just like her mother.

“We usually rely on Old Coal,” said Bert. “She can find anyone and anything in the whole wide world. Isn’t that right, Old Coal?”

“Aw! Aw!” answered the crow. She flew across the table and sat on Flora’s shoulder.

Flora fed the bird a tiny piece of meatball. “You’re such a smart crow. I wonder if you know how to swim.”

The Famous Flying Banana Brothers were already expert swimmers. They hit the diving board with gusto.

Barnabas Brambles was a strong swimmer, too. He jumped on the diving board, touched his toes, and then dived into the water, cutting it like a knife.

"You're next, Leo," said Flora. "And then Tiger."

Leo looked at Flora in disbelief. "But we're *cats*. We don't like water. We certainly can't be expected to swim."

"Mrraare mrraare," Tiger agreed.

Everyone should know how to swim. And believe it or not, lions in the wild can and *do* swim when necessary.
They *do*?
Mrraare?

"Yes, they do," said Flora. Then she lowered her voice and spoke more gently to the frightened felines. "I know you're both scared. But may I give you a swimming lesson? I promise I'll make it fun."

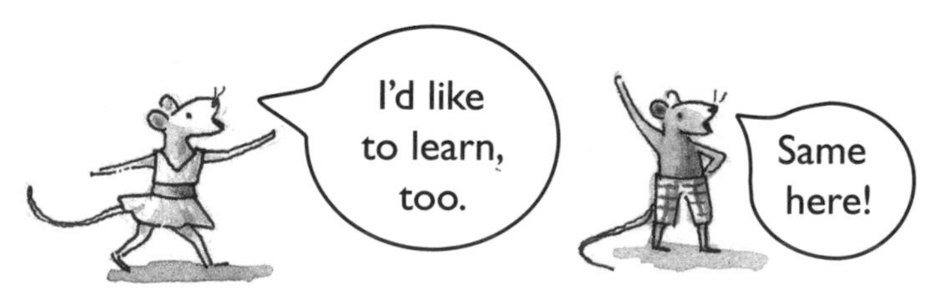

I'd like to learn, too.
Same here!

Soon, Leo and Tiger were dog-paddling—or *cat*-paddling—across the pool. Bert and Gert were right behind, *mouse*-paddling like mad.

If we were swimming in the ocean, I could *wave*.
Bert, please don't make me laugh! I'll get water in my whiskers!

"All right," Flora said at last to Elsa. "It's your turn."

Elsa frowned. She'd never been swimming in her life.

"Go on," yelled Leo from the other side of the pool. "You'll love it!"

"It really is a *lot* of fun," agreed Gert.

"Give it a try, Elsa," said Bert. "If *I* can swim, you can swim, too."

But Elsa shook her large head. A teardrop appeared in the corner of one eye. She tried to wipe away the tear with her trunk, but another tear was right behind it. She sniffled loudly.

I'm not as brave as the rest of you.
Oh, Elsa. It takes courage to admit you're afraid of something. I can teach you to swim. And once you learn how, it won't be so scary.

"Really?" asked Elsa.

"Really," said Flora. "You might be surprised to know that elephants are usually very good swimmers. They use their trunks as snorkels to breathe."

"They *do*?" asked Elsa.

"Yes," said Flora. "I bet you can do the same thing. But let's start from the beginning. The first thing I'll ask you to do is dip your toe in the water."

See?
You're a natural!

"What about me?" yelled Leo, who was practicing the backstroke.

Flora watched with pride as her students swam with confidence. Even Old Coal was using her wings to splash across the pool. Flora had taught her, too.

Meanwhile, Barnabas Brambles and the Famous Flying Banana Brothers were trying to top each other with fancy dives.

“Can you do this trick?” Barnabas Brambles asked as he bounced on the diving board. When he was high in the air, he touched his nose to his knees before plunging into the water.

“I can do that,” said Stan Banana. “Can you do this?” He bounced on the board and soared up, then turned, spinning like a top before gliding into the water.

"Anybody can do that," laughed Dan Banana. "Can you do this?" He jumped high on the diving board and then tucked his body into a ball before bursting like a firecracker into the water.

Elsa watched in awe. She climbed out of the water and walked over to the diving board.

"Elsa," said Flora carefully, "I'm not sure you should go on the diving board. Remember, you're still a beginner."

But Elsa wasn't listening. She stepped onto the diving board. She liked the way it moved under the weight of her heavy body.

Elsa began jumping on the diving board. She jumped higher and higher. The passengers who had been playing shuffleboard were gathering around the pool to watch the curious sight.

"Elsa," Flora said again in a nervous voice, "I'm not sure you should—"

But it was too late. Elsa took one final jump. While in midair, she yelled to the spectators.

Can you do *this*?

She landed in the pool with a spectacular splash. Every drop of water that was previously *in* the pool was now *out* of the pool. The shuffleboard players were soaked.

When Captain LaPasta heard the commotion, she came running.

Look what you've *done*!
Flora Endora Eliza LaBuena LaPasta, *now* do you see what a mistake it was to invite these creatures aboard the *Spaghetti*?

Flora didn't answer. She simply stared at her feet and tried not to smile.

Captain LaPasta took a deep breath and turned to face her customary customers. "The swimming pool is closed until further notice," she said.

"Why?" asked Mr. Slimskin. He and Mrs. Slimskin sailed on the *Spaghetti* several times a year.

"Because," Captain LaPasta announced, "I have no performers. My daughter fired them all."

Barnabas Brambles tapped Captain LaPasta on the shoulder. "Madam," he said, "may I point out that you have Sir Sidney's Circus on board? It's the best circus in the whole wide world."

"A *circus*?" cried Captain LaPasta. "Are you suggesting I let a common circus perform for my sophisticated guests?"

Barnabas Brambles smiled and nodded.

Captain LaPasta's eyes narrowed. "I don't need to *see* something to know I won't like it," she said. She then turned to speak to her paying passengers.

Please return to your cabins and dry off. I will ask Cookie to make extra spaghetti and meatballs for tonight's dinner. I hope that will make up for this inconvenience.

Elsa felt terrible about the mess she'd made. "I'm sorry," she said to Flora.

"Don't worry about it," Flora replied. "That was the most exciting thing that's happened on this ship in months—maybe even *years*. Just look at Mr. Marshmuffin and Mrs. Prunejam."

Flora was right. Even though they were soaked to the skin, Mr. Marshmuffin and Mrs. Prunejam were giggling like children.

Can you believe it? An *elephant* emptied the pool.
That was more thrilling than winning the shuffleboard championship!
I can't *wait* to tell the ladies back in Cincinnati about this.
I can't wait to swim again. It's wonderful exercise.
If swimming is such good exercise, explain whale blubber. *Whale?*

CHAPTER FOUR

On the second day at sea, Sir Sidney stayed in his cabin.

Bert and Gert were worried about him.

"Thank you," said Sir Sidney, who looked as miserable as he felt. "I'm too seasick to even read a book."

"How about a poem?" asked Gert. "I'll write a haiku for you."

A young girl at sea
Invites a circus to come
And be her first mate
That's a poem?
It's called a haiku. It's a three-line Japanese poem. The first and third lines have five syllables. The second line has seven syllables.

"It's a lovely haiku," said Sir Sidney. "But I think I'd better go back to sleep now. Will you please tell Barnabas Brambles I won't be able to teach him today?"

"Of course," said Gert.

"We'll tell him," said Bert.

The two mice scurried off to find Barnabas Brambles.

He was in the ship's library, gazing at a portrait of Captain LaPasta.

"Same thing," said Barnabas Brambles in a dreamy voice. "Isn't she amazing?"

Bert snorted. "The only amazing thing about our captain is that she hasn't thrown us all overboard yet."

"She would *never* do anything so heartless," said Barnabas Brambles.

"Maybe not," said Gert. "But it seems clear that Captain LaPasta doesn't like us."

Barnabas Brambles jumped to his feet.

Captain LaPasta might *think* she doesn't like us, but that's only because she doesn't *know* us. Once she gets to know Sir Sidney's Circus better, she'll like everyone in it, including me.
Don't get your hopes up.
Maybe you should write a poem for her. I could help you write an acrostic poem.

"Huh?" said Barnabas Brambles. "What's that?"

"In an acrostic poem, the first letters of each line are arranged vertically to form a word," said Gert. "Let me show you an example."

She borrowed a pen from Barnabas Brambles's pocket and wrote a simple acrostic poem on the back of an envelope.

Girl mouse
Everyone's friend
Really likes learning
Tries to be helpful
That's terrific! A poem is *exactly* what I need to impress Captain LaPasta.
Bert, do you want to help us compose an acrostic poem?
How many times do I have to tell you? I *don't* like poetry.
MY JOKES

Meanwhile, in the ship's kitchen, the Famous Flying Banana Brothers were talking to Cookie. He was busy making meatballs for the lunch buffet.

The Famous Flying Banana Brothers filled two large bowls with spaghetti and carried them out to the deck. They tied the strands of spaghetti together with knots. Then the twin brothers carried one long piece of rubbery pasta up the twin masts of the ship.

"Look!" said Leo. "Stan and Dan Banana are making a tightrope out of spaghetti."

"You don't think they're going to practice their tricks on a piece of pasta, do you?" asked Elsa.

Sure enough, five minutes later the Famous Flying Banana Brothers were performing acrobatics on a slippery strand of spaghetti.

"It's a good thing they're so light on their feet," said Elsa. "I'd hate to see them fall."

But the Famous Flying Banana Brothers didn't fall. They performed their potbelly-piggy-goes-to-the-parade trick perfectly.

Then came their laughing-leapfrog-double-loop trick.

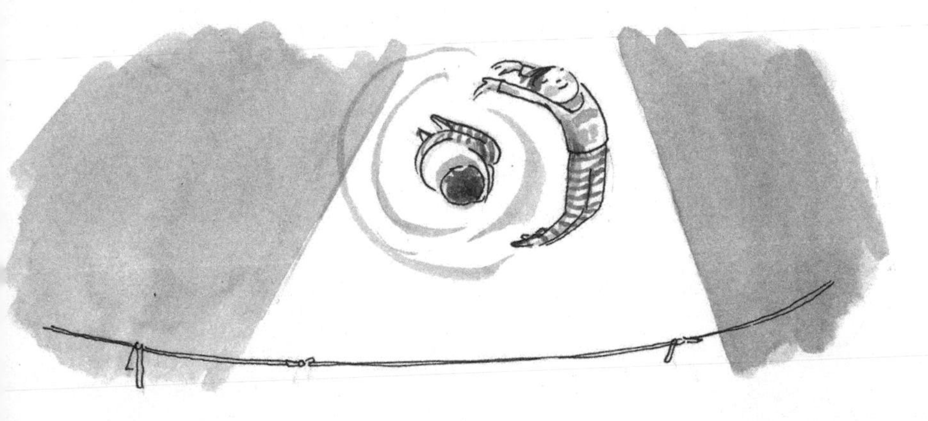

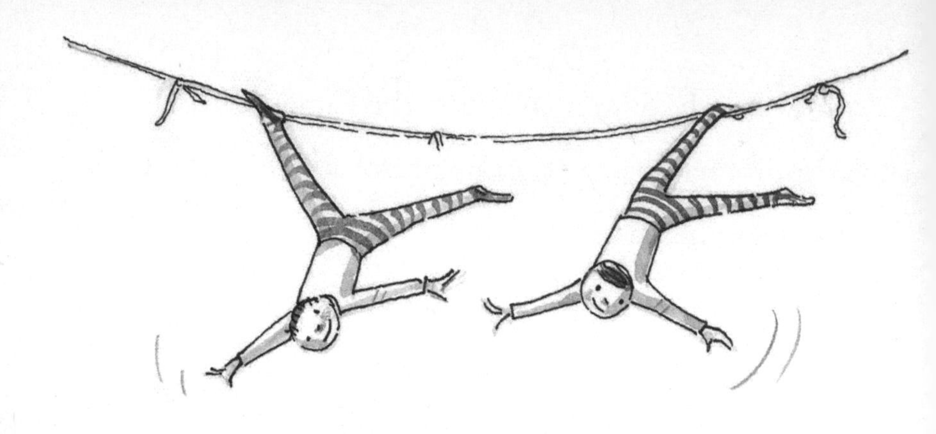

People were gathering below to watch.

"Boy, that looks like fun," said Mr. Slimskin. "I wish I had the courage to do tricks on a tightrope."

"But dear," said Mrs. Slimskin, "it's too dangerous."

"Maybe," said Mr. Slimskin. "But for some reason, I feel like trying something *new* today." He tapped Elsa's trunk. "Could you give me a lift? I'm not very heavy."

Mr. Slimskin rode Elsa's trunk up to the top of the mast until he was standing next to Stan and Dan Banana.

The Famous Flying Banana Brothers took turns tiptoeing across the spaghetti tightrope. Mr. Slimskin followed right behind.

Then the Famous Flying Banana Brothers practiced hopping on one foot across the spaghetti tightrope. Again, Mr. Slimskin followed right behind in fine form.

Then the Famous Flying Banana Brothers skipped backward across the spaghetti tightrope. Mr. Slimskin was surprised that he, too, could skip so well—and *backward* on a strand of spaghetti, no less. He couldn't resist looking down and waving at Mrs. Slimskin.

When he waved, he lost his balance. He fell off the tightrope and landed with a *thud* on Elsa's back.

"Are you all right, darling?" asked Mrs. Slimskin.

Mr. Slimskin nodded. "I think I bruised my bottom, but it was well worth it. What fun!"

When Captain LaPasta heard about the accident, she came running at once. "Who's in *charge* of this circus?"

Barnabas Brambles stepped forward. "Sir Sidney is the owner and founder, but he's not feeling well today. I am the assistant manager of Sir Sidney's Circus."

Captain LaPasta took one step closer and looked directly into Barnabas Brambles's eyes. She spoke slowly and with a scowl on her face, as if every word caused her intense pain.

Mr. Brambles, because of this circus, I have an empty swimming pool, an injured passenger, and *no* entertainment for my guests tonight.

It was the moment Barnabas Brambles had been waiting for. "Captain LaPasta," he said with pride, "allow *me* to help. Tonight, for the enjoyment of your passengers, I can recite my poetry. Let me show you an example of my work." He handed Captain LaPasta his acrostic poem.

Courageous
Always at sea
Proud to be boss
Tantalizing eyes
Amazing hair
Intelligent
Nice eyebrows, too

Lovely voice
Accomplished career wom
Pays attention to details
Assertive
Sophisticated
Tells it like it is
Always has clean teeth
and fresh breath

When Captain LaPasta finished reading the poem, her cheeks turned the slightest shade of pink.

I am
not immune to
compliments.
But really,
Mr. Brambles.

"Speaking," he replied sweetly.

"Kindly spare me your poetry," Captain LaPasta said.

"I was only trying to—"

Captain LaPasta interrupted. "We don't have time for such *nonsense*!"

Captain LaPasta turned to her daughter. "Flora Endora Eliza LaBuena LaPasta, *now* do you see what a mistake it was to invite this circus aboard the Spaghetti?"

But Flora didn't answer. She just smiled and watched her mother storm off in a huff.

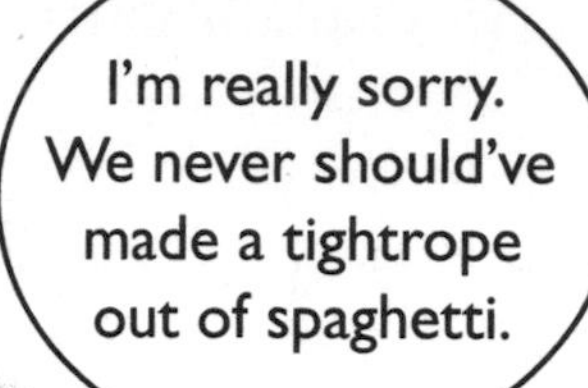

Flora shook her head. "I thought it was a *wonderful* performance," she said. "Everyone enjoyed it, especially Mr. Slimskin." She tipped her head toward the daring passenger, who was still beaming with pride.

I don't think I've *ever* felt more alive than when I hopped on one foot on a piece of pasta strung between twin masts on the SS *Spaghetti*.
I know *I've* never felt prouder.
This is truly the most exciting crossing we've ever made.
It certainly is. I can't wait to see what tomorrow brings!

They're *shore* enjoying this vacation.
Bert, that's another terrible sea joke.
Maybe you're getting *tide* of my jokes, but I'm having a *maritime*.
MY JOKES
SS SPAGHETTI

CHAPTER FIVE

On the third day of the voyage, it was impossible to see land. Many passengers enjoyed the mesmerizing beauty of the water. For them, the sound of waves lapping against the side of the *Spaghetti* was relaxing.

But the rocking motion of the ship made Sir Sidney's seasickness even worse. Once again, he was forced to cancel his daily lesson with Barnabas Brambles.

"I'm too sick to teach him anything," Sir Sidney said to Bert and Gert. "This will be a lost week in the education of Barnabas Brambles. Will you tell him for me, please?"

DO NOT DISTURB
Sir Sidney is sick.

FROM NEW YORK TO LONDON
168 hours
− 48 hours traveled so far
120 hours to go
No problem.
We'll tell him right away.

Barnabas Brambles was sorry to hear that Sir Sidney was still sick. "On the other hand," he said with a twinkle in his eye, "this gives me more time to think of a way to impress Captain LaPasta."

Over a breakfast of strawberry waffles, scrambled eggs, cinnamon toast, and hot cocoa, Barnabas Brambles explained his plan. "Consider this," he said. "Our captain has a lot on her mind. She's responsible for the safety and happiness of all her passengers. She's also concerned about the lack of nightly entertainment. So tonight we'll have a sing-along in the ship's ballroom."

"I *know* it is!" said Barnabas Brambles. "Now if you'll excuse me, I have a lot of work to do."

Barnabas Brambles spent the day preparing for the sing-along. He chose the songs and decorated the ballroom. He made posters. He wrote invitations using his neatest handwriting. Then he slipped an invitation under every cabin door.

Tonight's Entertainment

A Sing-along Aboard the SS *Spaghetti*

Don't miss an evening of fun and music!

Dress in your fanciest clothes and prepare to be impressed by Two Cool Cats named Leo and Tiger and other members of Sir Sidney's Circus, including Barnabas Brambles.

Location: Ballroom
Time: 7:00
Admission: Free
Please R.S.V.P.

Sir Sidney couldn't attend the sing-along.

R.S.V.P.

__ YES, I WILL ATTEND TONIGHT'S SING-ALONG.
X NO, I WILL NOT ATTEND TONIGHT'S SING-ALONG
BECAUSE I'm seasick.

Sir Sidney

Cookie couldn't come, either.

R.S.V.P.

__ YES, I WILL ATTEND TONIGHT'S SING-ALONG.
X NO, I WILL NOT ATTEND TONIGHT'S SING-ALONG
BECAUSE I'M BUSY MAKING MEATBALLS.

COOKIE

Captain LaPasta didn't reply to her invitation. But everyone else said they would come.

R.S.V.P.

X YES, I WILL ATTEND TONIGHT'S SING-ALONG.
__ NO, I WILL NOT ATTEND TONIGHT'S SING-ALONG
BECAUSE ______.

Tiger

R.S.V.P.

X YES, I WILL ATTEND TONIGHT'S SING-ALONG.
___ NO, I WILL NOT ATTEND TONIGHT'S SING-ALONG BECAUSE ________________.

Mrs. Prunejam

R.S.V.P.

X YES, I WILL ATTEND TONIGHT'S SING-ALONG.
___ NO, I WILL NOT ATTEND TONIGHT'S SING-ALONG BECAUSE ________________.

Elsa

R.S.V.P.

X YES, I ~~WILL~~ can't wait to ATTEND TONIGHT'S SING-ALONG.
___ NO, I WILL NOT ATTEND TONIGHT'S SING-ALONG BECAUSE ________________.

Flora

And come they did!

Dressed in ball gowns and tuxedos, they came and sang for two happy hours.

The sing-along was a great success.

Let's end with a song everyone loves. It's an old Scottish folk song called "My Bonnie Lies Over the Ocean."

My Bonnie lies over the ocean,
My Bonnie lies over the sea,
My Bonnie lies over the ocean,
Oh, bring back my Bonnie to me.

(Chorus)
Bring back, bring back,
Bring back my Bonnie to me, to me.
Bring back, bring back,
Oh, bring back my Bonnie to me.

On the final *me,* Leo and Tiger sang together in perfect harmony. Gert dashed up Leo's body and stood on the lion's shoulder, adding her own voice to the harmony.

When he saw his sister, Bert couldn't help himself. He raced up Leo's other shoulder and sang, too.

Mrs. Prunejam shrieked when she saw the singing mice. "Eeeeeeeeee!"

Mr. Slimskin shrieked even louder. "Oooooooooooooo!"

Captain LaPasta came running when she heard the screams. "What's going on here?" she demanded.

Barnabas Brambles beamed. "You're *just* in time, Captain," he said. He was thrilled she had decided to attend the sing-along after all.

But Captain LaPasta wasn't singing. She was boiling with anger.

You and your circus have emptied my swimming pool. You have injured one passenger. And now you have frightened my guests with *singing mice*!

"Oh, but I'm not frightened," stated Mrs. Prunejam. "Not in the least. I was shrieking from delight. I've never seen singing mice."

"Nor have I," said Mr. Marshmuffin. "What a treat! I must say, Captain LaPasta, this has been the most enjoyable crossing I've ever made."

Other passengers standing nearby added their praise.

Captain LaPasta couldn't believe her ears or eyes. Her passengers were smiling. They were *happy.* And it was all because of one man: Barnabas Brambles.

Captain LaPasta cleared her throat. "Mr. Brambles," she said, "it seems I was mistaken about you."

Barnabas Brambles smiled. "We all make mistakes."

Captain LaPasta raised her eyebrows. "But it's more than that," she said in a serious voice. "I owe you an apology. I thought you and your circus would ruin this voyage. Instead, you have provided my passengers with an evening of first-class entertainment. For that I am grateful."

She reached toward Barnabas Brambles to shake his hand. His heart turned a triple backflip as he extended his hand toward hers. They were within one inch of touching.

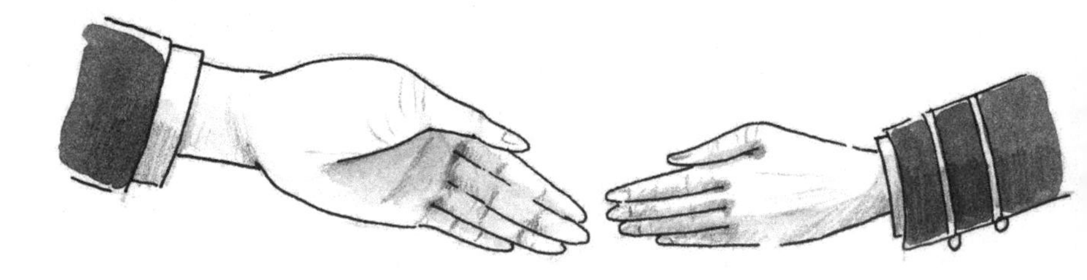

And that's when it happened.

The ship had slammed against something hard and cold. Captain LaPasta and Barnabas Brambles were thrown into each other's arms. Water was rushing in through a large gash in the side of the ballroom.

And the water was cold. Ice-cold.

"This is bad," said Gert. "This is *very* bad."

"Can you be more *Pacific*?" said Bert with a smirk.

"We're not in the Pacific!" squeaked Gert. "We're in the *Atlantic*!"

"Sorry." said Bert. "I was just trying to make a joke."

The SS *Spaghetti* had just hit an iceberg.

CHAPTER SIX

"Don't panic!" called Captain LaPasta.

But it was too late. As water flooded the ballroom, the passengers panicked.

"We'll *drown* if we stay here!" cried Mr. Marshmuffin.

"We must seek higher ground!" yelled Mrs. Prunejam.

"Up the stairs!" hollered Mrs. Slimskin.

"I'll lead the way," offered Mr. Slimskin.

But when they reached the bottom of the grand staircase, they found water rushing down the stairs toward them.

"It's hopeless," cried Captain LaPasta sadly. "We're surely sunk."

"I could write a tragic poem about this," said Gert, treading water. "But I don't think there's time."

"*Glug, glug, glug,*" replied Bert. He was not as strong a swimmer as his sister. He tried his best to stay afloat by *mouse*-paddling, but the icy water kept pulling him under.

Barnabas Brambles reached down and picked up Bert and Gert. He placed them safely in the pocket of his jacket. Then he made an announcement.

The frightened passengers nodded in agreement.

"Elsa," Barnabas Brambles said, pointing at the elephant, "you're a good swimmer. You have a trunk you can use as a snorkel. Please go find Sir Sidney and put him on your back. We want to make sure he's safe."

"Captain LaPasta," Barnabas Brambles continued, "please find Cookie and tell him to join us here. Ask him to bring the ingredients for meatballs."

"Meatballs?" asked Captain LaPasta. "Why meatballs?" She was up to her knees in water.

"Because I have an idea," said Barnabas Brambles with a wink.

When Cookie arrived, Barnabas Brambles explained his plan. "We must build a meatball big enough to patch the hole caused by the iceberg. If we all work together, we can do it. To make the job more enjoyable, let's sing while we work."

And so they did.

(Sing to the tune of "My Bonnie Lies Over the Ocean")

A meatball might save the *Spaghetti*.
A meatball might save us at sea.
A meatball might save the *Spaghetti*.
So please make a meatball for me.

(Chorus)
Make me, make me,
Please make a meatball for me, for me.
Make me, make me,
Oh, please make a meatball for me.

The meatball must be quite enormous.
The meatball must be very large.
The meatball we need now to save us
Must be twice as big as a barge.

(Chorus)
Make me, make me,
Please make a meatball for me, for me.
Make me, make me,
Oh, please make a meatball for me.

They built a giant meatball. It was not twice as big as a barge, but it was *really* big. Barnabas Brambles and Captain LaPasta worked side by side.

They rolled the meatball across the ballroom and wedged it tightly against the hole caused by the iceberg. Like a cork in a bottle, it worked. The meatball worked!

"We're not finished yet," said Barnabas Brambles. "Let's form a bucket brigade to get rid of all this water. We'll need everyone's help."

Passing buckets up the stairs and out to the deck, the circus members led the effort to return the ocean water its rightful place.

When they had finished, Captain LaPasta extended her hand to Barnabas Brambles for a second time that evening. “Mr. Brambles,” she said, “how can I ever thank you for saving the SS *Spaghetti*?”

Barnabas Brambles thought for a moment. Then, still holding Captain LaPasta's hand, he got down on one knee and sang a final verse of the sing-along song in a deep and tender voice.

A meatball just saved the *Spaghetti*.
A meatball just saved us at sea.
A meatball just saved the *Spaghetti*.
Oh, Captain, will you marry me?
Is he serious?
Goodness gracious!

Captain LaPasta lowered her voice. "Mr. Brambles, I've been married once before. It didn't turn out well."

Barnabas Brambles elbowed her in the ribs. "Where's your sense of adventure? Besides, I thought you didn't believe in looking back."

"I don't *ever* look back," Captain LaPasta said firmly. "But . . . but . . . but . . ."

"But what?" prodded Barnabas Brambles.

"My daughter doesn't like you," said Captain LaPasta. "She didn't even invite you on this voyage. Isn't that true, Flora?"

Flora bit her lip. "I made a mistake," she admitted.

"I listened to what other people said about him. I heard people say he was the meanest man alive. But it's not true. Barnabas Brambles is nice and funny. He's the first person who ever offered to be my friend. He's smart, too, and very brave. He saved my life."

"Mine, too," said Mr. Marshmuffin.

"He saved *everyone's* life," said Bert.

"He certainly did," said Sir Sidney.

"Now do you see what a good idea it was to invite a circus aboard the *Spaghetti*?" asked Flora.

Captain LaPasta smiled and kissed her daughter. "I *do* see. Thank you, my darling."

"I'm waiting for an answer," said Barnabas Brambles, tapping his foot.

Captain LaPasta turned to face him.

All right. I *will* marry you, Barnabas Brambles. Full steam ahead!
We're going to have a wedding! I must sew Mr. Brambles a new suit.
You could use those red-velvet curtains.
Good idea! I wish I had time to write a wedding poem, too. Maybe you could do that.
Oh *buoy*. This is really getting out of *sand*.

CHAPTER SEVEN

The wedding was held ten days later in London's Westminster Cathedral. Passengers from the SS *Spaghetti* and members of Sir Sidney's Circus filled the church. Friends and family came, too, including Elsa's cousin Louise, who lived in London. Captain LaPasta had sent all the fired entertainers plane tickets and invitations to return to their old jobs after the wedding, and they all came to join in the celebration.

Gert stayed up half the night sewing a wedding suit for the groom. She knew it was time well spent when she saw Barnabas Brambles standing at the front of the church in a red-velvet jacket and pants.

Isn't he a handsome groom? You're looking mighty handsome, too, Bert.
You *know* I hate getting dressed up. Whose idea was it for us to be flower mice, anyway?
Mine. Now here we go.

The wedding ceremony began with Bert and Gert. They walked side by side down the aisle, dropping flower petals and freshly popped popcorn.

"Nicely done," said Sir Sidney when Bert and Gert reached the front of the church. Sir Sidney was feeling much better now that he was back on solid ground. He was dressed in his best white suit because he was Barnabas Brambles's best man.

Next came Old Coal. She flew down the aisle carrying the wedding rings in her beak.

Flora was next. She wore a navy blue sailor dress and walked in front of her mother, who wore a beautiful white gown and carried a bouquet of seashells.

The minister spoke in a clear, calm voice. "Do you, Barnabas Brambles, take this woman to be your wedded wife, to have and to hold, in sickness and in health, in foul weather and in fair, whether seas are stormy or calm, from this day forward till death do you part?"

The minister turned to the bride. "Do you, Captain Astrid Amanda Miranda LaBuena LaPasta, take this man to be your wedded husband, to have and to hold, in sickness and in health, in foul weather and in fair, whether seas are stormy or calm, from this day forward till death do you part?"

The minister nodded. "If there is anyone present who objects to this union, speak now or forever hold your peace."

Barnabas Brambles turned to Sir Sidney. "If I marry Captain LaPasta, I'll have to quit my job with the circus so I can begin a new life at sea. Is that okay with you?"

"We'll find some way to manage without you," said Sir Sidney. "But I owe you an apology. I thought you could learn everything you needed to know by traveling with my circus. I was wrong. You learned more at sea."

Do *you* mind if I marry your mother?
Not a bit. It'll be great to have a friend at sea.

"But Flora," whispered Elsa, "there still won't be anyone your age aboard the *Spaghetti*."

"Or any cute, furry animals," added Leo.

"I know," said Flora. "But maybe you could all visit me once a year. Will you?"

Finally, Barnabas Brambles turned to Captain LaPasta. "Are you sure this is what you want, Astrid? If it is, I promise I will be your *best* first mate."

"You can't be that," said Captain LaPasta. "Leonardo LaPasta was my first mate. But you can be my *last* mate."

"That works for me," said Barnabas Brambles. He slipped a wedding ring on Captain LaPasta's left hand.

Once upon a time, I was known as the meanest man alive. Now I'm the luckiest man alive because I have found love. Circus life and love have made me a better man. *Padre*, let's seal the deal!

"Very well," said the minister. "By the authority vested in me, I now pronounce you husband and wife."

As the happy couple began to kiss, a strange idea popped into Bert's head. The idea became words. The words became rhymes.

Everyone in the church turned to stare at the mouse. But Bert only raised his voice and continued.

Gert elbowed her brother. "That's enough," she whispered.

But Bert ignored her. He climbed up Barnabas Brambles's red-velvet suit and stood on the groom's shoulder. Bert continued.

And this is true, for I don't josh, The man fed us goopy goulash!
Bert, please! This is a wedding!

"I can't stop. I'm on a roll!" Bert said to Gert. He kept on, his voice rising.

But then a glad thing did occur. This man I thought so bad met *her*.

Bert pointed at Captain LaPasta. Then he continued.

Every eyeball in the church was focused on Bert. Some passengers were taking out opera glasses to get a better look at the poetic little mouse.

"I'm sorry," said Bert, pausing to wipe away a tear that was trickling down his cheek. "What I'm trying to say is simple. I'm going to *miss* you, Barnabas Brambles."

Barnabas Brambles reached over and picked up Bert. "And I'll miss *you*, too," he said, holding the mouse in his hand. "Do you think we could still be friends?"

Forever. We'll *always* be friends.

Gert was watching all this in wide-eyed disbelief. "My brother said he didn't like poetry or lovey-dovey stuff. He certainly didn't like Barnabas Brambles. *Now* look at him."

Sir Sidney leaned down and gently scooped up Gert.

Life is full of surprises. Isn't it wonderful what can happen when you keep your heart open?
Good things happen when you keep your mind open, too.
And when you take a chance.
When you try something new.
When you find the courage to do something you've never done before.
When you follow your heart.
When you just dive in!

Everyone laughed, including Captain LaPasta. She cupped her hands around her mouth and made a loud announcement.

Attention, wedding guests! This is your captain speaking. The reception will begin promptly. Please make your way outside to the garden. Cookie has prepared a fine feast for us all.

What a feast it was.

Roast beef. Grilled salmon. Fried chicken. Shrimp cocktail. Cheese pizza. Mashed potatoes. Sweet potatoes. Cherry pie. Hot-fudge brownies. Twelve kinds of ice cream.

And, of course, there was spaghetti—*lots* of spaghetti—and a big wedding cake, too. Cookie had baked the cake in the shape of the SS *Spaghetti* and topped it with—*what else?*—a giant meatball.

CHAPTER EIGHT

It took a week for Sir Sidney's circus train to dry out. The engine was still damp from the iceberg incident. Traveling at top speed was impossible, so Sir Sidney drove the train slowly from London to a quiet village in the Cotswolds. It was the perfect place to rest after the adventure at sea.

"This might be a good time to discuss our schedule," said Sir Sidney. "As long as we're in England, would anyone like to visit the rest of Europe?" He held a map showing the proposed tour.

Let's do it!
EUROPE
N
W
E
S
I'd love to see Spain.
ENGLAND
FRANCE
SPAIN
ITALY
I bet our shows sell out in Italy.
France, too. Look. Paris, France, is located at latitude forty-nine degrees north and longitude two degrees east.

Sir Sidney wanted to ask Bert and Gert, too. He looked around for the little mice but couldn't find them. They were back in their mouse hole, unpacking their stamp-sized suitcases.

When Sir Sidney heard their voices, he bent down so that he could see inside the mouse hole. "Bert and Gert, does the idea of a European tour appeal to you?"

"Sure!" said Gert.

"Can we travel by train?" asked Bert.

"Yes," said Sir Sidney. "I don't think my stomach could handle another sea voyage."

Just then Old Coal arrived with a letter in her beak. It was addressed to Sir Sidney and Friends. Sir Sidney opened the envelope and read the letter out loud.

Flora Endora Eliza LaBuena LaPasta
Aboard the SS *Spaghetti*

November 20

Sir Sidney and Friends
Aboard the Sir Sidney Circus train
Somewhere in England

Dear All,

Thank you for coming to visit me. Not only did I get to see a circus, I made some wonderful friends, too.

Sir Sidney, I know sea travel is unpleasant for you. Maybe I could visit the circus once a year. Please write back and let me know what you think of my idea.

Your friend at sea,

Flora Endora Eliza LaBuena LaPasta

P.S. Barnabas Brambles wants me to ask if this is the end of the story.

Sir Sidney folded the letter and slipped it into his pocket. Then he bent down again to look inside the mouse hole. "Gert," he said, "is your typewriter wet?"

Gert put a piece of paper in the tiny machine.

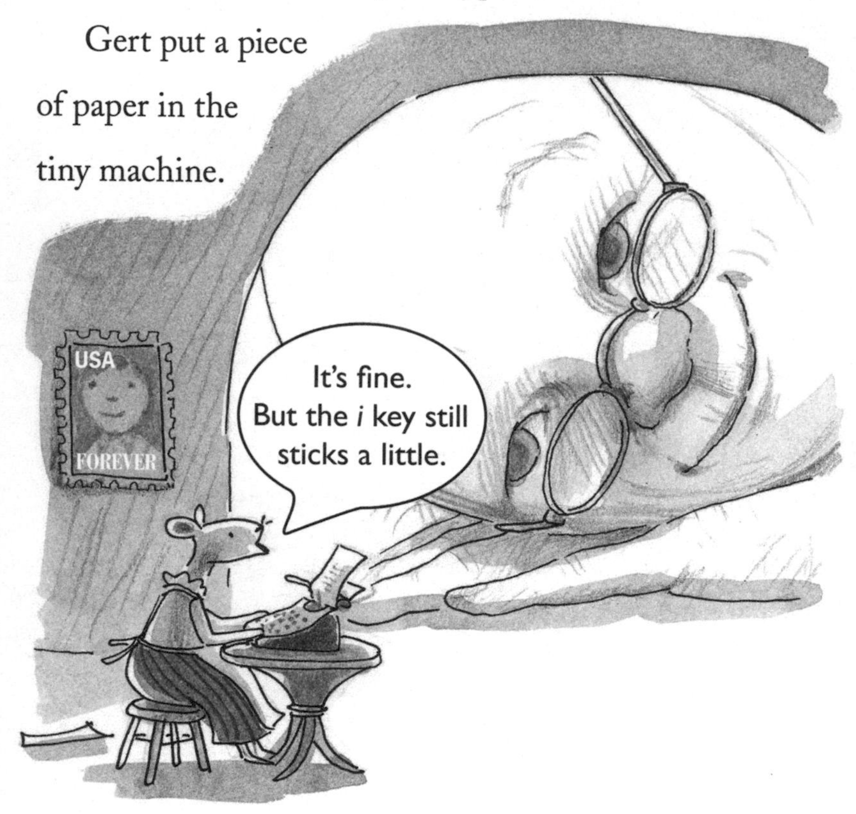

USA
FOREVER
It's fine.
But the *i* key still
sticks a little.

"That's okay," Sir Sidney said. "I'd like you to type a letter for me. Please address it to Flora Endora Eliza LaBuena LaPasta."

"Aboard the SS *Spaghetti*?" Gert asked.

"That's right," replied Sir Sidney.

The next day Old Coal delivered the letter to Flora.

SIR SIDNEY'S CIRCUS

Sir Sidney
Owner and Founder

November 21

Flora Endora Eliza LaBuena LaPasta
Aboard the SS *Spaghetti*

Dear Flora,

We thoroughly enjoyed our time aboard the SS *Spaghetti*. Thank you for inviting us.

You are always welcome at our circus. Come visit anytime. We'd love to see you.

Your friends forever,

Sir Sidney

Dan

Stan

Tiger

Old Coal

Gert

Bert

Elsa

Leo

"Look!" Flora said to her mother and Barnabas Brambles. "I just got a letter from Sir Sidney's Circus!"

"That's odd," said Barnabas Brambles, reading over Flora's shoulder. "Sir Sidney didn't answer my question."

Just then Old Coal circled overhead with another special delivery.

"Is that for us?" Captain LaPasta asked, looking up at the bird.

"Aw! Aw!" cried Old Coal as she gently dropped the paper into Flora's hands.

P.S. Please tell Barnabas Brambles
this isn't the end of our story.
It's only the beginning.

The End & The Beginning
Because after every show ends, another show begins.
Full steam ahead!

COMING SOON!

Three-Ring Rascals: Book 4

POP GOES THE CIRCUS!

MISSING

Have You Seen This Mouse?

No one can find the mischievous mouse named Bert. Sadly, Sir Sidney is forced to make a tough decision about the future of his circus.

Meanwhile, Bert is facing tough decisions of his own. Carried away by a balloon, Bert struggles to stay alive in a world filled with bad drivers, angry mobs, and greedy robbers. Luckily, Bert finds an old friend who has run away from home—in a most unusual way.

In the worst of times, a best friendship is born. But how long can a circus mouse and a runaway girl survive on their own?

Just when you thought all hope was lost,
Pop Goes the Circus!

ABOUT THE AUTHOR AND ILLUSTRATOR

KATE KLISE and **M. SARAH KLISE** are sisters who like to write (Kate) and draw (Sarah). They began making books when they were little girls who shared a bedroom in Peoria, Illinois. Kate now lives and writes in an old farmhouse on forty acres in the Missouri Ozarks. Sarah draws and dwells in a Victorian cottage in Berkeley, California. Together the Klise sisters have created more than twenty award-winning books for young readers. Their goal always is to make the kind of fun-to-read books they loved years ago when they were kids.

To learn more about the Klise sisters, visit their website: www.kateandsarahklise.com.

You might also enjoy visiting Sir Sidney and his friends at www.threeringrascals.com.